SHE IS LIVING POETRY

OKUHLE ESETHU

OE PUBLICATIONS

First published in South Africa in 2024 by

OE Publications

Copyright © Lindokuhle Esethu Hlatshwayo, 2024

ISBN 978-0-7961-4779-0

For more information visit: www.oepublications.com

SHE

IS

LIVING

POETRY

The poetry of life

One day,
I discovered words.
They didn't come knocking on my door.
I didn't stumble upon them
while walking along lonely and strange streets.

I discovered the poetry of life inside of me.
It was intertwined with my existence,
sewn into my skin,
a part of my soul.

It had always been, I realised.
I had just forgotten that I was a poet
at first breath.

That was the day I remembered to appreciate
the magic of my life.
That was the day I became fully alive.
That was the day I fell in love with my life.

Let the poetry of your times
live through you.

We are born storytellers
and learn how to be writers.

I want to be a writer.

I want to be a storyteller.

I want to be a performer.

I want to be a creative.

This is what will keep me alive.

This is what makes me feel alive.

This is what I love.

She is living poetry

I write to stay alive,
to feel alive.

When a day unfolds to its ending
and I have not written anything,
I feel as though I have not lived.

I need to constantly write myself alive.

The Artist's Way

Create.
Be human.

The human experience
is multilayered
yet simple.

Artists
are beings
who dare
to be fully human.

Creativity
is at the core
of our existence.

Art
for
me
is
like
an oxygen mask.

being an artist
is an act of bearing your soul
to the world
making your existence
a fragile experience

if you do nothing
if you do not create art
your life becomes meaningless

you feel as though
you are nothing
when you are not
being an artist

"So, what kind of artist are you?"

A shapeshifter.
The kind that allows herself
to be
whatever her soul
calls her
to be.

I write to feel the texture of life
through words.

To relive experiences.
To recreate life.
To reimagine the world.

I can't help but paint pictures with words.
This poetry makes the fabric of my life richer.

A gift from God

Let the ideas come
as they wish to come.

Let the ideas live
through you.

Your creativity is not yours.
It is a gift from God
for this world.

You are only the vessel.

Let God use you
to spread love
through this art.

I think being a writer
is a precious gift,
even when you are just living,
you are still writing…

The poetry of life writes itself
through your existence and experiences.

"What do you do for a living?"

I LIVE, LEARN, EXPLORE & CREATE.

**A creative:
Someone who explores, discovers and creates.

Creation of art.

The creation of art, for me, has always been
an indicative feature of being alive.
Creativity is at the core of being human.

At the end
of my life
I want to wholeheartedly say:

I'VE LIVED!
I was fully human.
I allowed myself
to feel every emotion,
to experience love, beauty and art.

I don't force these words out of me.
I simply exist and allow poetry
to intertwine with my existence
and clothe my life with beauty.

I spend time around nature, in solitude.
When I'm alone, in a quiet place,
I dive into the deepest crevices of myself
to explore the different parts of myself
and my creative capabilities.

When I'm around people,
I'm really with them,
paying attention to how they think, talk and live.

I write from everything and nothing.
The stories that inspire me are everywhere,
within and without.

Things that are making me
a better writer:

- Writing
- Reading
- Living
- Meditating
- Running in the morning
- Listening
- Watching movies
- Exploring
- Connecting to different frequencies
- Naps in the afternoon
- Love
- Prayer
- Allowing the poetry of life to write itself through my existence
- Being in harmony with life
- Appreciating art
- Boredom
- Silence
- Taking long walks
- Other people's stories

- Assuming the role of a writer
- Not writing

To write well, you have to live well.
Fully!

E.g. When you fall in love,
go all in,
to feel all the emotions
love has to offer,
so that even when love departs,
you are left with a scrapbook full of love poems.

The stories are everywhere.

Just step outside and step out of yourself.
Look into people's eyes when you talk to them.
Think up where the strangers are going
and where they come from.
Take off your earphones and listen to mothers
in taxis complaining about the weather and how
expensive surviving has become.
Pay attention to the grunts and grumbles of old men
who are tired from their meagre-paying work and cannot
wait to get home to drown their misery with beer.

A storyteller stays interested in the world around them.

But first, a writer is a reader.

A reader

Of

Books. People. Spaces. Movies. Experiences...

Stories are revealing of us.

Literature takes what is complex
and turns it into art,
which is less intimidating and more relatable.

Literature provides us with data graphics
of who we are and who we could become.

More than a poem

I am more than a poem.
I am love without boundaries.
I am drawn to stories and silences.

I can create darkness from nothingness.
I can also speckle the darkness
with stars that bring about brightness.

I am light.
I am God's art.
I am an artist.

I need time to myself.
To think. To not think. To write. To read.
To paint. To listen to the music in my heart.
To be myself. To learn myself.
To refigure myself. To quiet the world.
To slow down. To be grounded.
To make room for creativity and inspiration.
To just be.

My writing inspiration
usually comes
when I am bored.

Boredom is essential for creativity.

Make space
to do nothing,
to be nothing.

There are some dreary emotions
you should just be okay with.

That boring state called boredom,
for instance.

Learn to live with it.
Loneliness, too.

They are part of our nature
and the human experience.

Let boredom come and go,
like summer and winter.

Do not try to fill up those gaps.
There's no need to.

Allow yourself to be bored.

on the days when loneliness creeps in,
remember,
you have a library full of books.

books!
with words woven with sheets
that can sweep
that dull, unnecessary feeling away.

you do not have to travel far
to live
a vibrant life.
you do not have to travel at all.

I've lived many lives
by
reading, writing & performing.

For as long as I live

For as long as I breathe

Storytelling will always be a part of me.

Hold on
to the things
that keep you alive.

Hold on
to what makes you
feel alive.

When you visit words regularly,
they begin to live through you.

Fighting for survival

It helps to write from a selfish place.

Do not write for an audience.
Write what your soul calls to you to write.
Write your truth.
Write to stay alive.

Do not write what everyone else is writing.
Do not write what everyone else is asking you to write.

Write what you need to write.
How else do you plan on staying alive?

Write as though your life depends on it.
Because it does.

Writing from a place of trauma
can be an ironically traumatic experience.

Your triggers become your poetry prompts
and prompt you into facing yourself.

When you don't (face yourself; write from core wounds),
the trauma swells your body and causes blisters.

Let the ideas keep you up at night.

Let them haunt you during the day.

Let them consume you.

Let them become your obsession.

The birthing of an idea is a spiritual experience.

The steam from her coffee
rises with the sun.

Her lamp lights up
the poetry on her desk
as she begins to write herself alive.

I like writing like I am painting.
I intentionally break the conventional rules of literature
to paint pictures with my words.
Not just figuratively, but literally, too.

The structure and texture of this poetry
are designed to evoke emotion
before the words are even read.

Poetry is supposed to be fun.
Creative writing should set you free.

As a writer, immerse yourself in books.
Master the rules of literature.

Then, boldly break those rules!
Write like a painter.

Creativity

to create

you have to be unafraid of being yourself

you have to be willing to shed the shallow self

you have to be open
to discovering and recreating yourself

you have to give up the ego-self
and get beyond yourself.

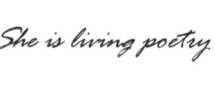

Creativity is a beautiful blossoming mystery flower.

Water it!

Discovering

reconnecting with your creative nature
feels like discovering a mystical world.

when you re-learn to live in that state,
you realise that creativity is a natural way
of being
that you forgot or abandoned along the way.

Creativity is a way of being.

Creator

You can spend your whole life chasing,
or you can use this precious time
that God has given you to create.

No matter what you choose,
know that nothing outside of you
will ever make you feel good about yourself.

So, create.
Live from the heART.

Storytellers
who dare to write
evolve
into writers
over time.

Keep writing bad scripts;
eventually, you'll evolve
into
a good writer.

Every great artist
starts out as an amateur,
just as babies crawl and fall
before they can walk and run.

Do not wait
any longer
to tell the stories that move you now.

We perceive the world differently
at different stages of our lives.
Thus, we retell different stories each time.

The story you write right now
will not be the same
when you revisit it later
because you will not be the same.

If you doubt that you are
a good writer,
write everyday,
write a lot,
write a lot everyday.

Write
until your pen
believes in you
more than you believe in yourself.

A duty to create

Any time you feel reluctant
to create,
remember that another artist
depends on
your art.

You feel the urge
to create
because you have been inspired
by another artist's art.

Therefore,
you have a duty
to the human race
to create,
to inspire other artists
to create.

How to always remain inspired to create:

Do not wait for inspiration.
Do not wait for motivation.
Create consistently.

Have routines, habits and systems
that make it easier for you
to create
without thinking too hard about it.

The only thing that makes a story bad
is the writer's lack of belief in it.

If you try to alter a story
because you feel compelled
by external influences
to turn your idea
into something it does not wish to be,
you kill it at infancy.

Write your stories

as they reveal themselves to you.

Be true to yourself and your stories.

Nobody knows the characters of a story
as well as the writer does.
Nobody knows the writer
like the characters she writes about.

For every story she tells,
a secret is revealed.
With each character she brings to life,
a part of her personality is explored.
Every plot twist and thrill
expose the depths of her heart and true nature.
Through the characters, by the characters,
the writer's essence is laid bare.

Without the writer,
the characters do not exist.
Without surrendering to the characters,
writing her truest truth,
the writer is not a writer.

So, there's no telling who holds the power.

HiStory

The histories
of my ancestors
have been silenced
for too long.

It's time
to revive
the spirit of storytelling
in my lineage.

When I write,
I keep certain characters alive,
I memorialise their lives.

When I pick and choose
what to write
based on my pride and prejudice,
I risk killing those begging
to not be forgotten.

Keep those forgotten alive!

Life begins.

Life ends.

That's it.

Life itself is a three-act structure:

We are born

We create art

We die

Her whole life is a creative act!

SHE IS LIVING POETRY!

ABOUT THE WRITER

Okuhle Esethu, legally known as Lindokuhle Esethu Hlatshwayo, is a visionary creative writer who paints with words. With a foundation in literature, film and drama, she holds a Bachelor of Arts degree with majors in Communications and Media and English Literature from the University of Johannesburg, and an Honours degree specialising in English Literature with a Scriptwriting minor from the University of Cape Town. Armed with a deep understanding of storytelling conventions, she fearlessly breaks the rules to ignite creativity in her writing.

She is living poetry!

www.ingramcontent.com/pod-product-compliance
Lightning Source LLC
Chambersburg PA
CBHW070809120626
46557CB00002B/780